Sarah the Spider
Prima Spiderina

Hilary Robinson · Illustration Jane Abbott

DRAGON'S WORLD
CHILDREN'S BOOKS

Sarah the Spider was famous at last,
The posters proclaimed that she had been cast
As 'Prima Spiderina – Star of the Show'
To dance in the barn, the quick-step and slow!

The big day drew near; with feathers and pearls
She worked on her steps, her spins and her twirls.
The crowd, she well knew, would be in for a treat
When they saw the new shoes on her eight pretty feet!

But they were a secret, all carefully hidden
In private locations with entry 'Forbidden',
So for now she made do with her old tatty shoes
And fixed them with buckles and rusty old screws.

Her talents for dancing were now on the map
For ballet and ballroom and modern and tap,
Who else could perform such an evening of dance?
With four pairs of legs – 'twas a spider's great chance!

The sheep built a stage from boxes and gates,
And old empty pots and rusty old crates,
The pigs set to work with needles and yarn
To make up some curtains with rags from the barn.

'I'll be the usher', cried Percy the Pig,
'That's easy for me, I'm burly and big,
The lambs might get trampled if there's a huge rush,
For the very front seats, there could be a crush.'

'And what of refreshments?', asked Old Mother Hen,
'We'll soon see to that,' offered Jennifer Wren,
'My birds will call out with loud chirps and tweets,
"Come get your choc-ices, cold drinks and sweets".

'We'll flutter around the seats at half-time
With cider and lemon juice, orange and lime,
And during the day we'll mix, make and bake
Sweet pastries and cookies and rich chocolate cake!'

The animals queued, their tickets held tightly,
The farmyard was lit by stars shining brightly,
One at a time they each took a seat,
On barrels of beer and sackfuls of wheat.

The scene was now set with everyone in
And Sarah rehearsed her kicks with a spin,
The moon lit the stage through a hole in the roof,
The spotlight was on; now, the moment of truth!

With a roll on the drum behind the haystack
Everyone gasped as the curtains drew back,
The audience clapped and whistled and cheered
But Sarah the Spider had not yet appeared!

The clapping soon stopped and so did the cheering,
They all stamped their feet and some started jeering,
Barney called 'ORDER!' and promised to see
Just exactly whatever the problem could be.

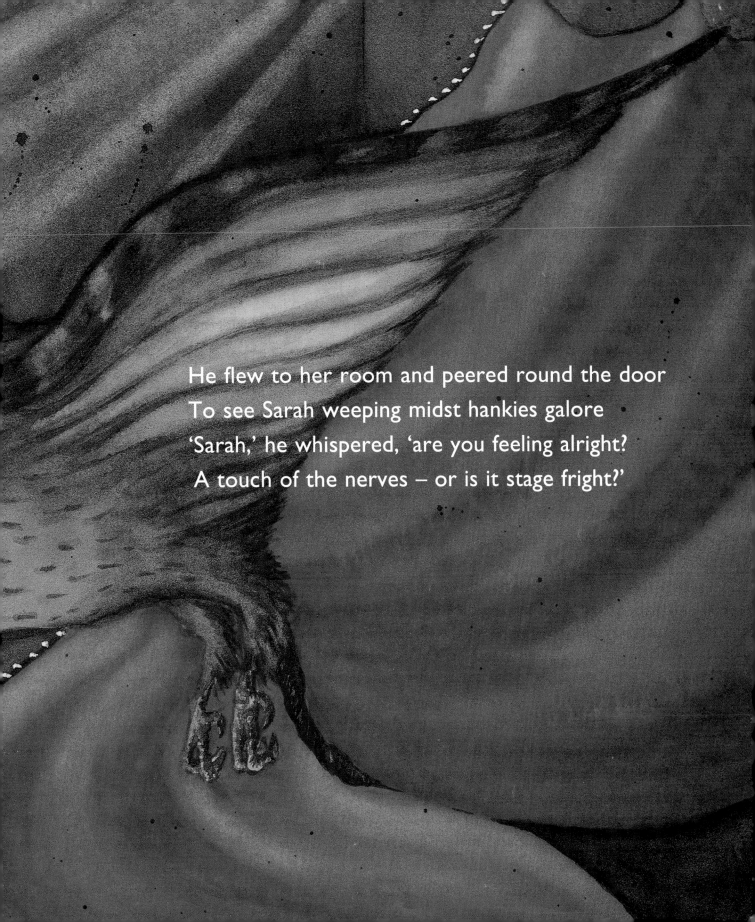

He flew to her room and peered round the door
To see Sarah weeping midst hankies galore
'Sarah,' he whispered, 'are you feeling alright?
A touch of the nerves – or is it stage fright?'

Sarah looked up, her eyes sore and misty,
'I can't dance,' she cried, 'my feet are all twisty!
Just look at what happens when I spin on the spot –
My legs become tangled, my feet are a knot!'

Barney pondered a moment, then nodded his head,
'Just walk to the door', he casually said.
She stumbled and fell, her shoes were so tight:
'Sarah! You've muddled your left and your right!'

Now it's not very often a spider turns pink,
But that's what can happen when owls start to think.
For they've wisdom enough to banish the blues
From sad, weepy spiders with ill-fitting shoes.

Barney Owl set to work with his principal claw,
And sorted the shoes into two sets of four –
Sarah now knew they'd no longer be tight,
With L on the left and R on the right!

Sarah ran to the stage and took up her pose,
As the music began, she pointed her toes,
With a cheer from the crowd she twirled round and round,
And spun in the air and tapped on the ground.

Without taking a break she danced on and on
In her magical shoes that sparkled and shone,
And to endless applause she danced through the night
As dusk turned to dawn and the dark turned to light.

Only eight-legged spiders can dance for long hours;
The stage by the end was covered with flowers!
Sarah curtseyed and bowed, she stifled a yawn –
Although she was tired, a star had been born!

DRAGON'S WORLD

CHILDREN'S BOOKS

Dragon's World Ltd
Limpsfield
Surrey RH8 0DY
Great Britain

First published by Dragon's World 1995

© Dragon's World 1995
© Verse: Hilary Robinson 1995
© Illustration: Jane Abbott 1995

The catalogue record for this book is available from the British Library

ISBN 1 85028 348 6

Editor: Kyla Barber
DTP: Keith Bambury
Art Director: John Strange
Editorial Director: Pippa Rubinstein

Printed in Bahrain